Night-Ti

Story—Eileen Pettigrew
Art—William Kimber

Annick Press, Toronto

Annick Press gratefully acknowledges the support of The Canada Council and the Ontario Arts Council.

Canadian Cataloguing in Publication Data

Pettigrew, Eileen, 1929–
  Night-time

ISBN 1-55037-235-1 (bound)   ISBN 1-55037-242-4 (pbk.)

I. Kimber, William, 1945–   . II. Title.

PS8581.E77N5   1992   jC813′.54   C92-093518-4
PZ7.P47Ni   1992

Distributed in Canada and the USA by:

Firefly Books Ltd.,
250 Sparks Avenue
Willowdale, Ontario
M2H 2S4

The art in this book has been rendered in water colour and pen-and-ink.
The text was set in Bookman light by Attic Typesetting Inc.

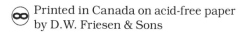 Printed in Canada on acid-free paper by D.W. Friesen & Sons

To the memory of my father

Michael liked to have his bedroom door open at night.

"I'm not afraid of the dark," he told his parents, "I just want to hear you talking downstairs."

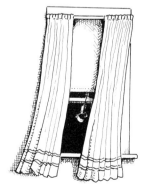

One night after supper, when he had had his bath, his father told him to put his rubber boots on over his pajamas because they were going for a walk and the grass would be wet from the afternoon rain.

They held hands going down the front steps. Far away someone was playing a guitar and people were singing. Michael and his father stopped to listen.

"Where are we going?" asked Michael.

"Let's see," his father replied.

They went along the path to the back yard. Everything seemed
dark and deep, like the velvet dress his mother sometimes wore
when she was going to a party. The sky was speckled with stars.

The only sound was a soft wind playing with the leaves of the old apple tree. Even the birds had gone to sleep. It was very different from daytime. Michael felt different too. With his father holding his hand he felt special and safe.

They stopped beside the lilac tree, and the sweet smell was all around them.

Near the fence Michael warned his father: "There's an anthill right there where you're going to walk. You should go around it because that's their house."

"You can see better in the dark than I can," his father said.

"That's because I play here all the time," Michael told him. "I know where everything is."

They walked a little farther, then Michael's father said:

"All around here was my father's farm when I was a little boy. Where the houses are now there used to be fields."

"Did you have horses and cows?" Michael asked.

"Oh, yes. Right next door where the Millers live was the barn. One night when I was just about your age my father came and got me out of bed to see a baby calf that had just been born. He carried me across the yard and there was the little baby standing up beside its mother. It was only a few minutes old and its legs were all wobbly."

He stood still for a minute, remembering. Then he said: "But that was a long time ago. Now there are houses everywhere."

"Will you carry me?" Michael asked.

"Sure," his father said. "You can sit on my shoulders."

"I wish this could still be a farm," Michael said. "I could have my own horse to ride."

Michael's father carried him up the steps to the wide verandah that ran all across the back of the house. Father sat down in the big brown wooden rocking chair and held Michael on his knee. They kept very still and listened to the whisper of the wind in the trees. Then they could hear another sound: Cree-oack, Cree-oack. "Those are tree toads," Michael said.

At last Michael began to feel sleepy. They went into the house and up the stairs. When his father tucked him in and kissed him goodnight, Michael said: "Maybe tomorrow you can shut my door."

"Not tonight?" his father asked.

"Maybe tomorrow," Michael said.

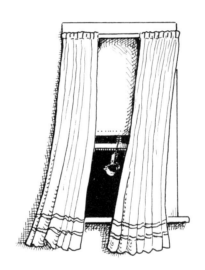